One · Two · Three How Many Animals Can You See?

ORCHARD BOOKS
96 Leonard Street, London EC2A 4RH
Orchard Books Australia
14 Mars Road, Lane Cove, NSW 2066
ISBN 1 85213 004 0 (hardback)
ISBN 1 85213 569 6 (paperback)
First published in Great Britain 1987
This paperback edition first published 1996

A CIP catalogue record for this book is available from the British Library.
Printed in Belgium

One · Two · Three How Many Animals Can You See?

ORCHARD BOOKS

One! Two! Three!
How many animals can you see?
Run, Rabbit, run!
That's just one!

1

Fox trots behind.
That makes two.

2

Duck paddles up.
That makes three.

3

Otter pops out.
That makes four.

4

Mouse joins in.
That makes five.

5

Owl flies above.
That makes six.

6

Hedgehog bobs along.
That makes seven.

7

Deer's waiting here.
That makes eight.

8

Squirrel scrambles on.
That makes nine.

9

One! Two! Three!
How many animals can you see?
Bear counts them all again.
Eight! Nine! Ten!

10

1 rabbit
1 fox
1 duck
1 otter
1 mouse
1 owl
1 hedgehog
1 deer
1 squirrel
+ 1 bear
10 animals

1
2 3
4 5 6
7 8 9 10